The Order Of The Eclipse

Eugene Halif, Volume 2

HooliewoodYella

Published by HooliewoodStudios LLC, 2024.

THE ORDER OF THE ECLIPSE

First edition. August 20, 2024.

ISBN: 979-8224995653

Written by HooliewoodYella.

Table of Contents

EUGENE HALIF: The Order Of The Eclipse

Prologue:

After spending hours at their favorite diner, Eugene and Marlon, both 12, stepped out into the embrace of the late summer evening. Their laughter echoed in the quiet streets of East Cleveland, a brief respite from the world's expectations. They decided to take the long way home, walking beside the train tracks that sliced through their neighborhood like a steel river. "Imagine if we followed these tracks out of Ohio," Marlon mused, kicking a pebble along the gravel. His voice carried a note of longing, a desire for adventures beyond the confines of their daily lives. Eugene picked up a stick, tracing it along the metal rails. "We'd see mountains, deserts... maybe even the ocean," he added, his imagination fueled by the stories they'd shared as they walked down the tracks.

Their path led them to a dirt Rock Hill

As they walk down the hill and enter

Alleyway, the familiar hum of the city faded behind them. They were in their own world, one of dreams and dares, until reality instantly shattered their sanctuary. Without warning, figures emerged from the shadows near the tracks, silent, swift, and intent on a singular purpose. Before Eugene could grasp what was happening, they had descended upon Marlon. There was no exchange, no demands, just the sudden, violent action of Marlon being ripped away from Eugene's side. Eugene screamed, a raw, desperate sound, but the figures paid him no heed. They were focused solely on Marlon, who struggled against their grip with a ferocity that belied his size. But it was futile. In moments, Marlon was dragged into the shadows from which the figures had emerged, disappearing from Eugene's life as quickly as they had entered it. The quiet that followed was suffocating. Alone and trembling beside the cold steel tracks, Eugene was paralyzed by shock and fear. What had just occurred was too much for his young mind to process. His friend, his brother in all but blood, had been taken, swallowed by the night.

Eugene wakes from the nightmare,

The early morning chill barely registered as Eugene jolted awake, the echoes of Marlon's screams still clawing at the edges of his consciousness. The nightmare had been vivid, a cruel replay of the day that had irrevocably altered the course of his life. He lay in the dark for a moment, his breath ragged, as if he had been running, fighting to reach Marlon before the shadows swallowed him.

The room felt oppressively silent, a stark contrast to the chaos of his dreams. Eugene swung his legs off the bed; the cold floor was a harsh reminder of reality. He couldn't shake the images, the sense of helplessness that haunted him. It wasn't just a memory; it was a festering wound that had driven him into the depths of East Cleveland's underworld.

He glanced at the clock—4:37 AM. Sleep was a luxury he could no longer afford, not with the shadows lengthening or the Order of the Eclipse lurking in every unseen corner of the city. The digital numbers blurred as Eugene rubbed his eyes, the weight of his crusade pressing down on him. Marlon's disappearance wasn't just a singular tragedy; it had become a beacon, drawing Eugene into a war he hadn't known existed.

Pulling on a pair of jeans and a hoodie, Eugene made his way to the small, cluttered space he had repurposed as a makeshift studio. The computer screen's glow cut through the darkness, casting long shadows across the room. This was where "Shadows of Babylon," his podcast, came to life. A project that had started as a desperate search for answers but had quickly evolved into something far more significant.

The familiar crackle of the microphone before him felt comforting as he sat, a semblance of control in the chaos. Yet, the words didn't come as easily as they used to. How many times could he recount the stories, the theories, and the near-misses without feeling the sting of his own failures?

Eugene pressed the record button, the red light flickering to life. "This is Eugene Halif," he began; his voice steady but tinged with an underlying fatigue. "And you're listening to 'Shadows of Babylon.' Today, we dive deeper into the abyss, seeking out the whispers of the lost, the cries of the forgotten. Today, we talk about the cost of seeking the truth in a city that thrives on secrets."

He paused; the silence heavy with unsaid words. This wasn't just another episode but a confession, a testament to the toll this journey had taken on him. "They say the night is darkest just before dawn. But what if dawn never comes? What if the night just... keeps getting darker?"

Eugene leaned closer to the microphone, his voice a raw whisper. "Marlon Wright was taken from us over a decade ago. Taken by Dark OTE shadows that I've been chasing ever since. This fight and quest for answers have cost me more than I ever thought possible. But I can't stop. I won't stop. Because the moment I do, the shadows win."

He pressed the record button, the room plunging back into silence. Eugene sat there, lost in thought, until the first light of dawn began to seep through the blinds. The battle against the shadows was far from over, and he knew that the path ahead was fraught with more danger and pain.

But he also knew that he wasn't alone in this fight. There were others out there who had been touched by the darkness and were willing to stand with him against the tide. Together, they would push back against the night, seeking out the light, however faint it might be.

And maybe, just maybe, they would find Marlon.

Eugene rose from his chair, the resolve hardening in his eyes. The day was beginning, and with it, another chance to challenge the darkness. With a deep, steadying breath, he stepped out of his studio and into the early morning light, ready to face whatever came next.

Chapter 1: The Order of Eclipse's

I met Cipher and his nascent coalition at an abandoned factory. The atmosphere is tense, underscored by the gravity of their undertaking. The abandoned factory loomed like a monolith against the grey sky; its skeletal remains were a testament to a bygone industrial era. As I approached, my boots crunched on the gravel, the desolate surroundings mirroring the desolation within him. This was where Cipher had called them together, a fitting place for those who operated in the shadows.

Inside, the vast, empty space amplified the sense of isolation. Pockets of dim light pierced the gloom, casting long shadows that danced on the walls. I spotted Cipher first, a silhouette against the backdrop of a rusted conveyor belt. The man was an enigma, a former detective turned rogue informant whose knowledge of the city's underbelly was unmatched.

Cipher nodded at my approach, his face an impassive mask. "Glad you could make it, Eugene," he said, voice gravelly with years of smoking.

Around them, the rest of the coalition emerged from the shadows, a motley crew bound by a shared vendetta against the Order of the Eclipse. There was Andria, her young face hardened by the disappearance and murder of her brother Shawn, her eyes burning with a fierce determination.

Rashid, the defector from the OTE, bore scars that told of his brutal past. Each carried their own story of pain and their reason for fighting.

And Amir, the youngest of the crew

Who I met while volunteering at a homeless shelter downtown

"We're all here," Cipher announced, his gaze sweeping over the group. "Thanks for coming. I know trust doesn't come easy, but it's our best weapon against the OTE."

I stepped forward, feeling the weight of leadership settle on my shoulders. "We're here because we've all lost something to the darkness," I began, my voice firm. "But together, we have a chance to fight back, to bring some light to this city."

Andria crossed her arms, her stance defiant. "And how do you propose we do that? The OTE is a hydra. We take down one head; two more spring up in its place."

Rashid stepped in; his voice rough but certain. "We hit them where it hurts. Their operations, their finances. We disrupt their network, create chaos."

Cipher nodded. "Exactly. But we need to be smart about it. I've been tracking their movements, intercepting messages. They're planning something big, something that could give us the leverage we need."

The group leaned in; the air charged with anticipation. Cipher laid out the plan, a series of coordinated strikes designed to cripple the OTE's operations in the city. It was ambitious, bordering on reckless, but it sparked a flame of hope in my heart.

"We'll need to split up and tackle multiple targets simultaneously," Cipher explained, pointing to a map of the city spread out on an old table. "Andria, I need you on surveillance. Rashid and Amir, y'all with me. We'll hit their financial hub. Eugene, you take the west docks. That's where they're smuggling in..."

The details flowed, and each assignment was handed out with precision. For a moment, I felt the enormity of our undertaking. We were outnumbered and outgunned but not outmatched in spirit.

As the meeting ended, I caught Andria's eye. There was a flicker of camaraderie there, a silent acknowledgment of the road ahead. "We've got this," I said, more to myself than to her.

Cipher clapped Eugene on the shoulder, a rare show of solidarity. "We start tonight. Be ready."

The coalition dispersed, melting back into the shadows they'd come from. I lingered, staring at the map. This was the beginning of our counterattack, the first real hope of striking a blow against the OTE.

The factory creaked around him, the sound echoing through the empty space. I turned and walked out into the fading light; the gathering shadows a cloak around him. Tonight, they would push back against the darkness. Tonight, they would fight.

And so, the stage was set, the players in motion. The battle lines were drawn, not just for me but for all those who had suffered at the hands of the OTE. In the heart of the city, amidst the ruins of industry and hope, a rebellion was brewing a storm of retribution against the encroaching night.

Chapter 2: Let the Hunting Begin

The coalition embarks on its first mission to disrupt an OTE operation. The action is intense and violent, showcasing my leadership and the group's collective might. Conflicts arise within the team, but they manage to succeed, signaling the first victory against the OTE.

The night air was charged with tension as my team, and I readied ourselves at posts off the Lake Erie docks.

The murky waters lapped quietly at the piers, unaware of the storm that was about to descend upon them. I surveyed my team, their faces masked, their bodies tensed for action. This was their first real test as a unified front against the Order of the Eclipse.

Cipher's intelligence had pinpointed tonight a significant shipment that would bolster the OTE's arsenal if allowed to reach its destination. Disrupting this operation could cripple their resources and send a clear message: the shadows were no longer safe for them.

My earpiece crackled to life, Cipher's voice grounding him in the moment. "Eugene, you're on point. Remember, we need that shipment destroyed, not intercepted. We can't afford to bring this fight to our doorstep."

Acknowledging with a curt nod, I signaled his team forward even though Cipher couldn't see Me. Stealth was their ally tonight. They moved as shadows among shadows, closing in on the warehouse that served as the OTE's staging ground.

Suddenly, a sharp hiss from Andria halted them. She gestured towards a pair of guards rounding the corner of the warehouse, their steps lazy, unsuspecting. Rashid moved, a silent specter, taking them down with swift, precise movements. The thud of bodies hitting the ground was soft, almost swallowed by the night.

They pressed on, reaching the warehouse doors. I took a moment to listen, the murmurs of voices inside reaching him. This was the heart of the beast, and they were about to strike. I exchanged a look with my team, and their unspoken bond was stronger than ever.

The breach was explosive, a cacophony of sound and fury as they burst into the warehouse. The OTE operatives inside were caught off guard, but their surprise quickly turned to resistance. A fierce firefight ensued, bullets tracing deadly paths through the air. I led from the front. My movements were deliberate and driven by a rage that was tempered by focus.

Andria and another team member, Amir, right of the crew, provided cover fire as Rashid and I advanced. The conflict was brutal, the air thick with the smell of gunpowder and the sharp tang of fear. Despite their training, the coalition was not immune to the chaos of battle. A misstep by Amir, driven by inexperience, nearly cost them dearly. I had to pull him back, a harsh whisper of reprimand lost amidst the gunfire.

"Focus! Don't let adrenaline make your choices!" My voice was a lifeline in the tumult, pulling Amir back from the brink of recklessness.

The OTE fought with the desperation of cornered animals. But the team was relentless, pushing forward until they reached the shipment.

The crates were marked with the OTE's insignia, a chilling reminder of the enemy they faced.

Cipher's voice was a constant presence in their ears, guiding them towards their objective amidst the chaos. "Left side, Eugene. Plant the charges there."

The battle raged around them as they secured the explosives, the tension mounting with each passing second. And then, with the detonator in my hand, they retreated, racing against time to escape the blast radius.

The explosion was a brilliant inferno in the night, consuming the shipment and sending shockwaves through the docks. The OTE's loss was palpable, a first victory that tasted of ash and smoke. As we regrouped in the shadows, panting and alive, the weight of their actions settled upon them. They had struck a blow, yes, but the night's events had exposed the fragility of their alliance. Conflicts had arisen, and decisions were questioned. I knew the path ahead would be fraught with more than just physical battles.

Yet, as they looked back at the burning warehouse, there was a sense of unity in their shared purpose. They had faced the darkness and emerged victorious, if not unscathed.

The hunt had begun, and the night was theirs. But as the flames reflected in my eyes, he understood the true cost of their war. This was but the first step in a long journey, one that would test them all to their very cores.

As I and the squad melted back into the night, the Lake Erie docks smoldering behind us, I felt the weight of leadership heavier than ever. The road ahead was uncertain, and the shadows were deep. But they had taken their first step into the fray, and there was no turning back now.

Chapter 3: Wake Up Call

The aftermath of the Lake Erie explosion had sent ripples through the city's underworld, a clear declaration of war against the Order of the Eclipse. But retaliation from the OTE was swift and merciless, a stark reminder that their adversary was both omnipresent and unforgiving. The first blow came under the cover of darkness, a favorite cloak for both predator and prey.

The safe house is a nondescript apartment in the heart of The Larchmere district, a historic commercial part of Cleveland known for its restaurants, art, and antique stores.

Had felt secure until the night it was breached.

We had been cautious, rotating locations and communicating through encrypted channels. Yet, the OTE had found them, a testament to their reach and resources.

The attack was brutal, a calculated strike meant to cripple and instill fear. We fought valiantly, repelling the assault. The echoes of gunfire barely faded before the reality of our situation sank in. We were no longer the hunters in this grim dance with the Order of the Eclipse; we had become the hunted. The attack on our safe house, a place I had foolishly considered secure, was a brutal wake-up call. We fought them off, yeah, but at a cost. Amir was badly wounded; the young 18-year-old that was raised in foster care who thought he could change the world, now bearing a scar that would forever remind him of the cost of our crusade. The weight of our decisions hung heavy in the air.

After the chaos, as we patched up Amir's wound, the room was thick with tension, and each of us was lost in our thoughts. The silence was punctuated only by Amir's pained breaths.

I couldn't help but feel responsible. These people had joined my fight and were now paying the price.

"We can't let them just hit us like that," Andria murmured, the strain evident in her voice. Her words, laced with unspoken fear, cut through me. She was right, of course. This was a war of attrition we seemed destined to lose.

I snapped back, more harshly than I intended. "Then we make sure we're the ones doing the hitting." My voice sounded foreign to my ears, fueled by a mix of anger and desperation. We had known the risks, yet facing the consequences head-on was a different beast altogether.

And Rashid, with his unwavering resolve, added fuel to our simmering fury. "And we hit them back harder." His determination was infectious, a reminder of why we had embarked on this path.

In the silence that followed, I realized the abyss we stood before wasn't just a physical threat; it was the potential loss of ourselves and the danger of becoming what we sought to destroy. The scars we bore were a testament to our battles, but the unseen wounds threatened to undo us.

The days after were a blur of motion and paranoia. We moved from one hideout to another, ghosts drifting through the city. Amir's recovery was a slow, painful reminder of our vulnerabilities, a constant shadow that trailed our every step. The threat of another attack loomed over us, a silent specter that kept us on edge.

Despite the fear and the constant danger, it was the resolve I saw in my team that kept me going. We were battered, yes, haunted by the scars of our encounters, but not defeated. The fight had taken so much from us, yet something stronger had been forged in its fires. A bond, unbreakable and fierce, born of shared pain and purpose.

One night, looking into the faces of those who had become my family, I felt a surge of resolve. "We're in this together," I said, my voice echoing in the sparse room. The words were a pledge, a vow that no matter the darkness that awaited us,

We would face it as one. "We won't break. We can't. We're all we've got, and we're not going anywhere."

As we prepared to step back into the shadows to continue our fight against the OTE, I realized that the abyss wasn't something to fear. It was a challenge to be met, a darkness to be illuminated by the light we carried within us. The road ahead was uncertain and fraught with peril, but we would walk it together, defiant in the face of the night.

The retaliations hit us harder than expected; they attacked every hideout spot that we had. It's like they always had eyes on us, and the OTE was making it clear they were not just shadows; they were a tempest. Our so-called safe houses, once a fortress in our minds, had proven to be nothing more than a paper shield against their might.

Yet, as we regrouped, licking our wounds and plotting our next move, we knew we were missing a crucial piece of the puzzle: the faces and names of those who pulled the OTE's strings. It was time to unmask our enemy, I said. But this time, we're going after the kingpins orchestrating this madness," I declared, my voice light in the darkness that had settled over our latest hideout.

Cipher had come through, his network of informants and surveillance tapping into the OTE's communications. He laid out the Intel, photos, and dossiers of the OTE's top brass spread across the table like a deck of sinister cards.

First, there was Vincent

Barelli, "His vision had shaped the OTE into the monstrous entity it had become. His ability to stay in the shadows, a whisper of a man whose designs were felt but seldom seen, made him a prime target.

Next to him was Sam McNamara, the "Enforcer." His methods were brutal, her network of enforcers the clenched fist of the OTE, crushing any who opposed their agenda. His reputation preceded him, tales of ruthlessness that chilled her blood.

And then there was Dominic Rothschild, the "Banker." He was the lifeblood of their operations, his financial acumen ensuring the OTE's endeavors were well-funded and its coffers overflowing. Cutting off their financial pipeline would cripple them significantly.

"We hit them hard, disrupt their command structure, and throw their operations into disarray," I plotted, finger tracing the lines connecting these key players on the map before us.

Rashid nodded his expression grim but determined. "It's time they learned to fear."

Her resolve reignited. Andria added, "Let's bring the fight to their doorstep."

Despite being battered and bruised from the safe house attack; Amir insisted on being part of the action. "I'm in. They need to pay."

As we when are separate ways into the night, the weight of our mission bore down on us. We were no longer just fighting the shadowy limbs of the OTE; we were striking at its heart, challenging those who believed themselves untouchable.

The hunt for the OTE's top members had begun, and with it, a new chapter in our war against the darkness.

Chapter 4: Rothschild The Banker

The night was quieter than usual, the city holding its breath as if sensing the storm brewing in its underbelly. Cipher's latest Intel had led us down a path none of us expected: a trail of breadcrumbs that hinted at a sinister connection between Marlon's disappearance and the OTE's shadowy machinations.

It was in the hushed confines of an abandoned warehouse, the air thick with the scent of decay, that Andria, Rashid, Amir, and I pored over the files Cipher had unearthed. Each document, each photo, whispered secrets of a sprawling network dedicated to the unthinkable: child abductions.

"The OTE's involved in this trafficking ring?" Andria's voice was a mix of horror and disbelief, her eyes scanning the damning evidence spread out before us.

Rashid's jaw was set, his usual stoicism giving way to a palpable rage. "Looks like they've been using these... operations as a front for their activities. Funding their cause with the lives of the innocent."

I couldn't help but feel a surge of guilt and responsibility. Marlon's face, forever etched in my memory, constantly reminded me why we'd started this fight. But now, the stakes were higher, the enemy more monstrous than we'd imagined.

"We need to take this to the authorities," Amir suggested, his youthful optimism clashing with the grim reality of our vigilante crusade.

"And risk exposing ourselves?

No, we handle this our way,"

I countered the weight of leadership heavy on my shoulders. "There's a name here, someone who could lead us straight to the heart of this operation. Dominic Rothschild."

The "Banker." His involvement provided the missing link, the financial thread weaving through the tapestry of the OTE's darker enterprises. It was decided we'd strike at Rothschild, dismantling this part of the OTE's network and avenging the lives torn apart by their greed.

The confrontation with Rothschild was inevitable, a clash forged in the fires of our resolve. We tracked him to a secluded estate on the outskirts of the city, the kind of place that reeked of ill-gotten wealth and secrets.

The estate loomed before us; a fortress of corruption veiled in opulence. As we approached under the cloak of darkness, the silence was punctured by the crunch of gravel underfoot, a harbinger of the violence to come. We split up, Andria and Amir circling to flank the main entrance while Rashid and I prepared to breach.

Rashid nodded at me, the unspoken language of brothers-in-arms. "On your go, Eugene."

I kicked at the door, the force of years of pent-up rage behind the blow sending it flying off its hinges. We stormed in, the element of surprise momentarily ours until gunfire greeted us, the estate's opulent interior exploding into chaos.

"Down!" I shouted as bullets whizzed past, embedding into the rich mahogany and priceless artworks that lined the foyer. We returned fire, a symphony of gunfire that filled the expansive hall.

Andria's voice crackled through the comm, a mix of concentration and fury. "We've got company!" She was calm under fire, her shots calculated, and each one finding its mark among the enforcers who poured into the hall.

Rashid grunted, a bullet grazing his arm. "Just a scratch!" he yelled back, his voice a mix of pain and adrenaline. He dove behind a statue, firing off a series of shots that took down two more enforcers.

I caught sight of Rothschild, the "Banker," at the far end of the hall, his expression one of shock that quickly morphed into malice. "You think you can take me down; you ghetto trash?!" he bellowed, arrogance dripping from every syllable as he fired in our direction.

The room was a maelstrom of destruction, bullets and shouts filling the air. I maneuvered through the chaos, every step bringing me closer to Rothschild. Our eyes locked, and at that moment, there was a silent acknowledgment of the reckoning that was upon him.

Rashid covered me, his gunfire a relentless barrage that kept Rothschild's guards at bay. "Eugene, now!" He shouted the opening clear.

I charged at Rothschild, dodging his desperate shots, the distance between us disappearing with each heartbeat. We collided with the force of colliding storms, the fight turning hand-to-hand, and a primal battle for survival.

Rothschild was hillbilly strong, his punches fueled by desperation, but the righteousness of our cause lent me strength. I countered his blows, finding openings in his defense, each strike a message.

"This is for the lives you've ruined!" I snarled, my fist connecting with his jaw in a satisfying crunch. Rothschild staggered, the fight draining from him as the realization of his defeat sank in.

The room fell silent, the echoes of our battle hanging heavy in the air. Andria and Amir emerged, their expressions a mix of relief and weariness. Rashid joined my side, his gaze on the fallen Rothschild.

Pale but resolute, Amir stepped forward, his voice steady despite his evident pain. "You're done, Rothschild. The OTE's reign ends with you."

Rothschild spat blood, his defeated gaze flickering with a hint of fear.

"You think you've won? The OTE is bigger than me, bigger than anything you can imagine."

As we secured Rothschild, ready to leave the shattered remnants of his empire behind, the cost of our victory weighed heavily upon us. Amir's earlier wound had reopened in the fray, a stark reminder of the stakes.

"We need to get him looked at," Andria said, concerned about etching her features as she supported Amir.

The night air was cooler as we stepped outside, and the estate behind us was a symbol of our resolve. Yet, as we made our way back to the shadows from which we'd come, I couldn't shake Rothschild's words. The fight was far from over; we'd merely scratched the surface.

But as I glanced at my companions, their determination unyielding despite the odds, I knew we'd face whatever came next together. We were more than a team; we were a family forged in the fires of adversity, ready to stand against the darkness, no matter what horrors it held.

Chapter 5: Feathers Get Ruffled

The dust had barely settled from our raid on Rothschild's estate when the cracks within our coalition began to show.

We were back in our makeshift command center, an abandoned warehouse that felt more like a crypt in the cold light of dawn. Amir's injury was a glaring reminder of the cost of our crusade, a silent specter that hovered over us all.

"I can't believe you let Amir go in like that," Andria snapped, her frustration breaking the tense silence. "He was hurt, Eugene. We should have pulled back."

Her words stung, not because they were unjust but because I felt the weight of every decision I had made. Leadership had never felt so heavy, and the balance between aggression and caution was never so fine.

Rashid leaned against a graffitied wall, his arms folded, and his expression unreadable. "Andria's right. We played right into their hands. We got lucky this time."

"Lucky?" I retorted, my patience fraying. "We took down a key player in their operation. We knew the risks going in."

"It's not about the risk!" Andria shot back, her eyes blazing. "It's about recklessness. Amir could have died because we didn't think it through."

The air crackled with tension, every word a spark threatening to ignite the powder keg we'd become. Amir, ever the peacemaker, tried to interject, his voice weak from pain and exhaustion. "Guys, stop. It's not Eugene's fault. I chose to go in."

His words did little to quell the storm. The truth was, we were all fraying at the edges, the constant pressure and fear chipping away at our resolve.

Cipher, who had remained silent, finally spoke, his voice cutting through the heated exchange with calm authority. "This infighting is exactly what the OTE wants. They're counting on us to fall apart."

His words were a bucket of cold water, dousing the flames of our discord. He was right. Our unity was our strength; without it, we were just individuals waiting to be picked off.

"We need to be smarter," I said, taking a deep breath, trying to find the leader within me that seemed so elusive. "Andria, Rashid, you're both right. We've been operating on adrenaline, reacting instead of planning. We can't afford any more mistakes."

I looked at each of my team members, seeing their weight and the sacrifices they had made to stand by my side. "We're all that stand between the OTE and their complete control over this city. We can't lose sight of that. We can't lose sight of why we started this fight."

The room was silent, the air thick with unsaid thoughts and lingering resentments. It was Andria who broke the silence, her voice softer now. "We need to trust each other. We can't do this alone."

Rashid nodded a silent concession. "Let's focus on what's ahead. We have a long fight in front of us."

I knew the road ahead would be fraught with more dangers and decisions that could fracture our fragile alliance. But as I looked at my team, at the people who had become my family, I knew we had something the OTE could never break: our bond.

"We move forward together," I affirmed, my voice steady. "We learn from our mistakes, we adapt, and we keep fighting. Not as individuals, but as a coalition."

The rifts within us were real, the resolutions hard-fought. But in that moment, we understood that our unity was our greatest weapon against the darkness that sought to engulf us. We were battered, yes, but unbroken. And as the sun rose over the city, casting long shadows across the warehouse, I knew we could face whatever lay ahead together.

This was our crucible, and we would emerge stronger from its fires.

Chapter 6: Heat of the Night

I received intelligence about a secret OTE facility where abducted children are held. The group plans a daring raid. Cipher relayed the intelligence that would steer us into the abyss once more, a secret facility in a sundown town on the outskirts of Cincinnati, a den where the OTE held their youngest captives. The revelation was a gut punch, the reality of our enemy's depravity sinking in like a knife. My mind raced; haunted by the possibility that Marlon could've been among those imprisoned here when he was taken.

"We hit them tonight," I declared, the weight of command heavy in my voice. The room was a crucible of resolve, the air thick with the promise of retribution.

Rashid and Andria nodded; their faces set in grim determination. Amir, still recovering but fueled by a fire that not even his injuries could dampen, insisted on joining. "I'm in. I won't stand by while those kids are in danger," he said, his voice hard as steel. The plan was audacious, a direct assault on the facility under the veil of darkness. We knew the risks, but the stakes of innocent lives demanded action.

The night enshrouded everything in its embrace, transforming the abandoned warehouse on Miles Ave into a realm of shadows and silence. There, against the backdrop of forgotten structures, our bus stood a spectral figure in midnight blue, its quiet presence a testament to the mission at hand.

As I gripped the keys to our transformed vehicle, I felt the weight of the past and purpose. This bus, meticulously outfitted for our dangerous endeavors, represented more than a mere means of transport; it was a sanctuary of safety in the darkness, a pillar of hope for those we aimed to rescue.

My team assembled in the soft glow spilling from the bus's interior, each member a vital piece of the mosaic we formed together. Andria, with her martial artist's grace, radiated a serene readiness. Rashid, our tower of strength, stood vigilant. Young Amir, his youthful determination shaped by a challenging upbringing, looked on with resolve.

Then there was Cipher, leaning nonchalantly against the bus, his gaze meeting mine. Cipher was the only one who had been with me since the beginning of this crusade. His raspy voice carried our history in every word. His technical genius, a guiding light in our darkest moments, had been crucial to our survival and success.

The memories of why I embarked on this path surged within me, as vivid as the day they were seared into my heart. When I was twelve, the world I knew shattered in a single moment as my best friend was taken from me and kidnapped in broad daylight. That loss, that moment of utter helplessness forged my resolve. It transformed my grief into a commitment that no one else would suffer such a fate if I had any say in it.

Turning to face my team, I felt a surge of shared purpose. "This bus, cloaked in the night, represents much more than our mode of transportation. It embodies our unwavering commitment to those we seek to save. Armed with the lessons from our past and the strength of our unity, we're here to keep our promise to protect and offer hope."

As we boarded the bus, a collective determination enveloped us. We each found our place, surrounded by the high-tech gear that kept us one step ahead and the space we had meticulously arranged for those we would rescue. Cipher's presence beside me was a constant reminder of our shared history, a grounding force as we faced the uncertain future.

With a turn of the key, the bus's engine came to life, its hum soft yet full of promise, symbolizing the strength and resilience that had become our hallmark. As we pulled away from the warehouse district, our midnight blue guardian blended into the night, ready to face whatever challenges lay ahead. Driven by a resolve born from a deep-seated loss and fueled by the bonds forged on this journey, we set out to make a difference, one rescue mission at a time.

Cloaked by night, after a long 4-hour Drive, we approached the facility, a fortress of concrete and steel that stood as a monument to the OTE's cruelty. Andria and Amir, moving like shadows, disabled the perimeter cameras, their movements precise, silent. Rashid and I cut through the fence. The facility was like the old Mansfield prison, its halls echoing with despair's soft, haunting sounds. Our steps were cautious, and the tension was a tangible force driving us forward. The element of surprise was our only ally, and we wielded it with precision.

We reached the holding area, the air thick with the scent of fear and hopelessness. The captives' eyes, wide with terror, met ours as we burst into the room. "It's okay. We're here to get you out," I whispered my voice a beacon of hope in the pervasive darkness.

The rescue was swift, each of us moving with purpose, unshackling the children from their bonds. Andria, her heart a well of compassion, comforted them, her presence a soothing balm to their fractured spirits.

But as we ushered the captives out, our escape was fraught with danger, the facility now a hornet's nest of alarm and chaos. The OTE guards roused to defense, unleashed a torrent of gunfire that tore through the silence of the night.

"We need to move now!" Rashid barked, returning fire as we navigated the maze of corridors. The children, frightened yet resilient, followed their trust in us a heavy responsibility we bore with honor.

The battle was fierce, an eruption of violence that tested our limits. Amir, despite his earlier injuries, shielded a group of children with his body, his bravery a stark contrast to the cowardice of their captors.

Andria, her marksmanship unparalleled, took down guard after guard, her shots a whisper of death that spoke of her unwavering resolve.

Rashid, a juggernaut of fury, fought with a ferocity that matched the tempest in his heart, each blow delivered in the name of the innocents who had suffered at the hands of the OTE. And I, driven by a rage that bordered on recklessness, pushed forward, the specter of Marlon's disappearance fueling my every move.

The night air greeted us as we broke free from the confines of the facility, the stars above witnesses to our defiance. The captives, now safe in our care, were a testament to the righteousness of our cause.

Yet, as we vanished into the night, the facility ablaze in the chaos of our making, the victory felt hollow. Marlon remained lost to me; his fate was a question mark that loomed large in my mind. The raid on the OTE facility was a message, a declaration that we would not stand idly by while innocents suffered. But it was also a reminder of the journey ahead, of the battles yet to be fought and the mysteries yet to be unraveled.

As the dawn approached, casting the night into memory, the heat of the night had forged us stronger, but the path ahead was fraught with uncertainty. We would continue our mission to fight the evil that preys on the weak, our resolve unyielding, our spirits undeterred by the mysteries that lay in wait.

Chapter 7: Light of the night

The city awoke to chaos. The news of the raid on the OTE's child-holding facility had spread like wildfire,

It was a beautiful sight to see all of their families reunite with their children. A light of hope for some, a call to arms for others. But for us, it marked the beginning of a relentless backlash. The wounded and furious OTE unleashed their wrath upon the city, their sights set squarely on us.

We moved like phantoms through Ohio, always one step ahead of the encroaching danger, or so we hoped. But the OTE was everywhere, their influence seeping into the very fabric of the urban landscape we called home. It wasn't long before we found ourselves embroiled in a series of confrontations that tested our resolve, endurance, and will to fight.

One such encounter found us in the shadowed maze of an abandoned construction site, the skeletal remains of what was meant to be a haven of prosperity now serving as the backdrop for our urban warfare.

"Contact left!" Andria shouted her voice cutting through the din of gunfire and the crumbling of concrete under the force of bullets.

I pivoted, firing in the direction of her warning, the recoil of my gun a familiar comfort in my hands. Rashid was beside me, a steady presence in the eye of the storm, his shots precise, a testament to his unyielding resolve.

Amir, though still nursing wounds from our last encounter, fought with a ferocity born of necessity, his determination undimmed by the pain that shadowed his every move.

The OTE came at us with everything they had, their numbers seemingly endless, a tide of malice and destruction. We fought back with equal intensity, and every action was a declaration of our refusal to be broken.

In the chaos, a moment of dread froze me to the core. Andria, moving to cover Amir's flank, was caught in the open as a grenade arced through the air, landing with a malevolent his mere feet from her.

Time slowed as I lunged towards her, every instinct screaming to get her out of harm's way. The explosion rocked the foundation of the building, a deafening roar that sent us tumbling through the air, a maelstrom of dust and debris enveloping us.

When the world righted itself, I was on the ground, Andria beside me. Her eyes were wide, shock and pain etched into her features, but she was alive. Alive.

"We need to move!" Rashid's voice, laced with urgency, cut through my relief. He was right. We couldn't afford to stay, to give the OTE any more opportunities to claim us.

We retreated a tactical withdrawal into the labyrinthine heart of the city, the sounds of our adversaries' frustrated shouts and gunfire a fading echo behind us.

The cost of our escape was high. Andria was hurt, a shard of shrapnel, a cruel reminder of the narrow line between life and death we walked every day. Amir's earlier injuries were exacerbated, his resilience a thin veneer over the grimace of pain that he couldn't quite hide.

As we regrouped in the relative safety of another temporary hideout, the weight of our situation settled over us like a shroud. We were being hunted, pushed to our limits, and the city we sought to protect was becoming a battlefield.

Andria's injury was a stark illustration of the price of our war. The line between sacrifice and recklessness had blurred, and I questioned our chosen path. Was our fight doing more harm than good? Were we saving the city, or were we contributing to its destruction?

But as I looked into the eyes of my team and saw the resolve that burned there despite the odds, I knew there was no turning back. We had set ourselves against the darkness and would see this through, no matter the cost.

Our personal sacrifices were etched into our very souls, a testament to our commitment to the cause. The path ahead was uncertain, fraught with danger at every turn. Yet, despite the chaos and the brutality of our urban warfare, we remained united, our resolve hardened by the battles we had faced.

We were more than a team; we were a family forged in the crucible of conflict, ready to stand against the tide to fight for a city that teetered on the brink of darkness. The cost of war was high, but the price of inaction, of allowing the OTE to claim the city, was higher still.

We would endure, persevere, and emerge from the chaos not as victims, but as victors. The battle for the city's soul was under attack, and we were its last line of defense.

Chapter 8: The Family Rat

In the aftermath of our skirmish with the OTE, the quiet that enveloped us was more than just the absence of noise; it was the calm before the storm, the silence that screams.

A few days later, I called a private meeting with Adrian and Amir

We meet up at one of our new hideout spots in Outhwaite Homes, a public housing project located in the 5th Ward district of Cleveland,

It was here that I broke the news that Cipher had betrayed us

Cipher had been the backbone of our intelligence, the eyes and ears that guided us through the shadowy OTE operations. His betrayal was not a wound; it was an amputation, leaving us crippled and exposed.

"I don't understand... Why?" Andria's voice was a mix of rage and heartbreak, her fierce spirit unable to comprehend the depth of Cipher's deception.

The revelation was a gut punch to each of us, but it was a devastating blow for Amir. Raised in the unforgiving system of foster care, Amir had learned early on that trust was a luxury, one that had to be earned and could easily be broken. Yet, in us, he'd found something akin to a family, a sense of belonging that had always eluded him. Cipher's betrayal was not just a personal affront but a demolition of the fragile foundation upon which Amir had built his trust.

I watched Amir as he processed

Cipher's betrayal, the lines of confusion and sorrow etching deep across his youthful face. It was a stark reminder of the stakes of our struggle, not just in the physical battles we waged but in the war for the hearts and minds of those who had chosen to stand with us.

"We need to act," I said, the weight of leadership never heavier upon me. "Cipher's betrayal cannot go unanswered. We protect our own, and we end this,

We decided to meet cipher at

The warehouse on Miles, its dark silhouette, is in stark contrast to the night sky. Inside, the air was thick with anticipation, charged like the calm before a storm. Cipher stood across from us, the embodiment of our deepest betrayal. His once familiar features were now etched with the lines of defiance and cold calculation.

The sting of his deceit was a gash across the heart of our coalition, but no one felt it more keenly than me. Cipher had been the first to join this fight alongside me, a brother in arms in what now seemed like another lifetime. His betrayal didn't just break trust; it sought to dismantle the very foundation we'd built together.

"Cipher, out of everyone, you were the last person I expected this from," I found myself saying, my voice a mix of disbelief and anger. "We started this together. You stood by me when we had nothing but a shared goal."

How could you?" My voice echoed off the high ceilings, the hurt, and disbelief in my words as palpable as the tension in the air.

Cipher's smirk was a dagger to the heart. "How? Because Eugene, believing in ideals is a luxury we can't afford in this city. The OTE offers power and protection. Your little rebellion was doomed from the start."

Rashid stepped forward, his presence imposing despite the wear of countless battles. "We trusted you, Cipher. You were supposed to fight with us, not against us."

Andria and Amir flanked me, their readiness visible in their stances, a silent testament to our unity in the face of betrayal. The atmosphere was a tinderbox waiting for a spark.

Cipher laughed a sound that sent shivers down my spine. "Trust? In this game, trust is a weakness. You'll learn that if you survive."

That was the spark. The warehouse erupted into chaos as Cipher's allies emerged from the shadows, their sudden appearance a well-orchestrated trap. Gunfire filled the air, a cacophony of death that danced around us.

We dove for cover, returning fire with practiced efficiency. "Amir, Andria, with me! Rashid, cover our flank!" I shouted, coordinating our response on the fly.

Andria's response was a symphony of gunfire, her shots precise and deadly. "Cipher! This ends tonight!" she yelled, her voice a mix of rage and determination.

Young but fierce, Amir moved like a shadow, using the warehouse's clutter to his advantage. His movements were a blur, a dance of survival as he made his way closer to Cipher.

Ever the immovable force, Rashid laid down a barrage of fire that kept Cipher's goons at bay, his every shot a promise of retribution. "You're not walking away from this, Cipher!" he bellowed, his loyalty to our cause as unwavering as ever.

Cipher fought back with a desperation born of cornered ambition, his movements slick and dangerous. But it was clear he had underestimated the bond that held us together; the resolve forged through battles fought side by side.

The battle was fierce, the warehouse a maze of gunfire and peril. Andria took a hit, a graze that was too close for comfort, but she pressed on, her resolve unshaken. In a daring move, Amir managed to disarm one of Cipher's men, using the enemy's weapon against them.

I focused on Cipher, our paths inevitably converging amidst the chaos.

"You could have stood with us, Cipher! You chose this path!" I yelled over the din, our final confrontation unavoidable.

Cipher met me in the center of the warehouse, the eye of the storm. "Eugene, you're a fool if you think you can change anything in this city," he spat, launching himself at me.

Our clash was brutal, a culmination of betrayal and broken trust. Cipher was skilled, but my anger and my sense of betrayal fueled my strikes, giving me the edge. We traded blows, the sound of flesh and bone, and a harsh melody in the deadly orchestra of the warehouse.

In the end, it is Cipher's arrogance that leads to his downfall. A misstep, a moment's overreach, and I had him. The fight drained from his eyes, but there was no remorse, no plea for mercy.

The decision to end Cipher's threat was made in silence, an unspoken agreement among us. As I stood over him, the reality of what we were about to do weighed heavily on my soul. But it was necessary. For the city, for our future, for the innocents caught in the crossfire of this war.

Cipher's end was swift, a final act in the tragic play of our once shared ideals. As we walked away from the warehouse, the weight of what had transpired settled over us. We had survived. The night air was cool on my face, a bittersweet reminder of the fragility of our cause. But as I looked at Rashid, Andria, and Amir, I knew our resolve was stronger than ever. Cipher's betrayal had tested us, but it had not broken us. The fight against the OTE would go on, and our bond would be a testament to the strength of our convictions.

"We move forward," I said, my voice steady despite the tumult of emotions within. "Together."

And so, we stepped into the darkness, united in our purpose, ready for whatever battles lay ahead. The war was far from over, but we were ready, our spirits unyielded, our resolve unbroken. The night might have brought to light the deepest betrayal we'd faced, but it also reaffirmed the strength of our unity and purpose. Cipher's final gambit failed not because of his lack of planning or our superior skills but because he underestimated the power of loyalty and shared convictions. In the end, those were our true weapons, ones no amount of manipulation or deceit could overcome.

As we walked away from the warehouse wreckage, the early hints of dawn painted the sky a soft gray, a new day rising on the horizon. It symbolized a beginning, a chance to renew our fight with the clarity and purpose that Cipher's betrayal had momentarily clouded.

Amir's steps were firm beside me, a silent statement of his resilience. Cipher's betrayal is a profound blow to him. Yet, there he was, moving forward, his determination a clear sign that while trust can be shattered, the human spirit's capacity to heal and fight remains indomitable.

Andria, nursing her wound, her expression a mix of pain and resolve, was a testament to the sacrifices we were willing to make. Her dedication, unwavering even in the face of personal injury, served as a stark reminder of the costs of our battle and its necessity.

Rashid, his presence a comforting constant, looked toward the rising sun, his gaze contemplative. "What Cipher did... it will not define us. We define ourselves through our actions and our choices. We keep fighting, not just against the OTE but for the city we believe can exist beyond this war."

His words resonated with each step we took, leaving the shadow of the warehouse and Cipher's betrayal behind. The city was waking up, unaware of the battle that had been fought in its underbelly. Yet, for us, the war continued; each day, there was a new fight, and each battle was a step closer to the peace we sought to achieve.

The path ahead was uncertain, fraught with more challenges and possibly more betrayals. But as I looked at my companions, my friends, I knew we were ready. Ready to face whatever came our way, to stand up against the darkness with the bright light of our conviction.

Cipher's betrayal was a scar on our collective heart, but it also served as a catalyst, strengthening our resolve. In the end, we were more than a team; we were a family, bound not by blood but by a common goal and a shared belief in a cause greater than ourselves.

We faced it head-on together. And in that unity, we found our strength, hope, and resolve to keep fighting until the end.

Chapter 9: Life after Betrayal

In the aftermath of Cipher's betrayal, the nights grew longer for me. I found myself pacing the remnants of our hideout, now nothing more than a mausoleum of their former certainties. The team's morale had fractured, with whispers of doubt and betrayal poisoning the air they breathed. Yet, amid the turmoil, a sliver of hope flickered a lead on the OTE's plans that hinted at a connection far more insidious than anything we'd encountered before. Amir, Rashid, Andria, and I gathered around, their expressions a mix of weariness and resolve. I spread out a map, its surface littered with pins and strings tracing the veins of the OTE's influence through the city and beyond.

We've been caught in an endless game of catch-up for too long; it's time we cut off all the heads," I stated, my finger hovering over a cluster of pins on the east side.

"I've got intel on a major operation happening here. This isn't just about drugs or guns; it's something that ties them to a network stretching across the damn globe."

The room tensed at the revelation. Their fight was ballooning, shadows lengthening into an ominous dusk that threatened to swallow them whole.

Rashid leaned in; his brow furrowed. "You're talking about expanding our scope, hitting them where it hurts before we even clean up our backyard?"

I met his gaze, the weight of command settling heavily on my shoulders. "Yes. If we take out this node, we cripple their operations here and start unraveling their network. We need to be strategic, hit them hard and fast."

Andria's voice cut in. "And what if this leads us straight into a trap? We're not exactly operating at full strength, Eugene."

Her concern echoed around the room; a sentiment shared by all. Yet, the fire in my eyes was undiminished. "It's a risk, but one we have to take. We can't keep reacting; it's time we set the terms of this war."

We need to tear down the OTE and anyone connected to them. This operation is our best shot."

The team exchanged looks; the decision unspoken but unanimously understood. We were in too deep to back out now, our path set towards a confrontation that would test their limits.

As we prepared, I received an anonymous message, its contents sending a chill down his spine. "Be careful who you trust," it read a warning or a threat that left more questions than answers.

The night was silent as they geared up, the darkness before dawn oppressive. Yet, as we moved out, a sense of unity fortified their resolve.

Cipher's betrayal only made us.

More vicious. Bound by loss, fury, and the unyielding desire for justice.

We would face whatever came our way together, forging ahead into the darkness until we saw the light.

Chapter: 10 The Broker

The raid was a calculated dance of shadows and gunfire; every move was choreographed under my precise commands. We descended upon the OTE's operation with the ferocity of a storm, striking hard and fast, a testament to their resolve. The warehouse, a labyrinth of contraband and whispers of far-reaching crimes, became the battleground for their assault.

Inside, amid the chaos of their surprise attack,

I spotted the target, a low-level operator known to be the linchpin in the OTE's latest venture. The team moved with practiced efficiency, cutting through the ranks of surprised OTE soldiers, their actions synchronized under the cover of night.

As the dust settled, with the enemy subdued or scattered, I gaze fixed on the captured operative, a young man whose eyes flickered with fear and defiance. Rashid dragged him to a dimly lit corner of the building, the aftermath of their raid echoing around us.

"Why are you doing this? Do you think you can stop it? Stop us?" The operative sneered, his bravado unconvincing in the face of his capture.

I leaned in, my voice low and steady. "Tell us about The Broker. What's being planned?"

The mention of The Broker elicited a flicker of surprise in the man's eyes, betraying his fear. Rashid tightened his grip, a silent threat that they were not in the mood for games.

"The Broker... You have no idea what you're stepping into," the operative whispered, a mixture of fear and awe in his voice. "He's the link... between the OTE and... and them." He trailed off, unwilling or unable to say more.

I exchanged a look with Andria, who was meticulously scanning documents seized from an office. "Eugene, you need to see this," she called, holding up a piece of paper with a list of dates and cryptic references. "It's bigger than we thought. This isn't just about the city anymore."

Their captive laughed a hollow sound. "You think your hunters, but you're just another prey in the game," he said, echoing the earlier message I had received.

Ignoring him, I focused on Andria's findings. "This... The Broker's meeting is next week. Not just him; it's a gathering of their entire network."

The revelation sent a wave of adrenaline through me. This was their chance, a rare opportunity to strike at the heart of the network that had ensnared their city and perhaps even find leads on Marlon.

But the risks were monumental. An operation of this scale against an unknown enemy with ties stretching beyond their borders was daunting. The shadows we fought against were growing longer and more dangerous.

As we prepared to leave, the warehouse was a testament to their resolve, and my mind raced with the implications of our discovery. The web was indeed widening, ensnaring them in a global conspiracy that threatened to overwhelm their local crusade.

Yet, as the crew and I stepped out into the night, we felt an unspoken bond tighten among us. We were no longer just fighting for their city; we were now embroiled in a battle that spanned beyond any borders they had known.

The drive back was silent; each lost in their thoughts about the implications of their raid. I knew the decision to pursue The Broker was fraught with danger, but it was a path I had to take. For Marlon, for their city, and now, it seemed, for much more than that.

The night gave way to the first light of dawn as they returned to their hideout, the city unaware of the shadows that moved with purpose through its streets. I looked at my team, their faces set in determination, ready for the war that awaited them.

"We dive into the unknown, "I finally said, breaking the silence. "But we do it together. For all those lost to the wickedness of the OTE doings. We bring the fight to them."

And with that, we stepped into the widening web, unaware of the eyes that watched us from the darkness, calculating, waiting. The game was changing, and they were now players on a much larger board.

Chapter 11: The Architect

As we huddled in the dimly lit confines of our latest hideout, the shadows seemed to cling a little tighter, a physical manifestation of the threat that loomed over us. The Architect, a name that had surfaced increasingly in the whispered rumors of the underworld, was no longer a faceless specter. He was Hoover Nixon, a man whose benign appearance belied the ruthless strategist within. With a demeanor as cold and calculated as his plans for the city's domination, Nixon had stepped into the power vacuum we had created, consolidating the OTE's fractured remnants under his chillingly efficient leadership.

The attack on our hideout had Nixon's signature written all over it, a bold declaration that he was not merely content to operate in the shadows but was intent on crushing any opposition. His former military strategist background gave him an edge that we had not anticipated, making him a formidable adversary.

And then there was The Broker, the enigmatic figure whose reach extended far beyond the city's borders. Information had revealed him to be Donald Reagan, a man of wealth and influence who thrived in the grey areas between legality and criminality. His network was vast, a tangled web of connections that spanned continents, facilitating everything from arms dealing to human trafficking. Reagan's involvement meant that our fight had escalated to a global stage, a daunting realization that weighed heavily on us.

As we sat in the stifling silence, Rashid broke the tension. "Nixon is making his move. He's not just aiming to control the city; he's reshaping it in his image. We need to act and fast."

Andria, nursing her wound, her voice laced with pain and determination, added, "Reagan is the key. If we can disrupt his operations, we cut off Reagan's support. It's a long shot, but it might just give us the edge we need."

"We focus on taking down Nixon first, I started. Nixon is here, in our city, threatening everything we stand for. As for Reagan, we'll need allies and resources. It's going to take everything we have and more."

The team nodded; a silent pact forged in the dim light. The battle lines were drawn, not just for the soul of the city but for the very lives caught in the crossfire of our war.

"We'll need a plan," I said, my mind racing with the enormity of the task ahead. "Nixon won't expect us to come at him directly after the attack. It's risky, but it might be our best chance to catch him off guard."

"And Reagan?" Andria asked, her gaze sharp.

I met her eyes, the resolve in my own reflecting back at me. "We start building our network, reaching out to those who have fought against him. It's time they were brought into the light."

The path forward was fraught with danger, a labyrinthine journey that would test us in ways we had yet to imagine. Hoover, Nixon, and Donald Reagan had become the faces of our adversaries, embodiments of the corruption and greed we sought to eradicate. The battle for the city, for the very essence of what we fought for, was about to intensify.

As we prepared to step back into the fray, I realized that this was more than a fight for justice; it was a crusade against the darkness that sought to envelop everything we held dear. We were no longer just defenders of the city; we were warriors for the light, determined to break the chains that Nixon and Reagan sought to impose.

And so, with the names and faces of our villains etched into our minds, we stepped out into the night, ready to face whatever came our way. The fight was personal, the stakes higher than ever. But together, we stood united in a light of hope in the encroaching darkness.

Chapter 12: Hoover Nixon

The chill of the pre-dawn air was a stark contrast to the fire that burned within us as we prepared for the assault on Hoover Nixon's stronghold. Nestled in the heart of the city, his fortress of corruption was a testament to the blurred lines between legality and criminality under his command. This was more than a raid; it was a declaration of war against the darkness Nixon had brought upon the city.

As we navigated through the deserted streets, the city seemed to hold its breath, anticipating the outcome of a battle that would herald a new dawn or further descent into chaos. The simplicity of our plan belied the complexity of its execution: infiltrate Nixon's base, neutralize him, and disrupt the web of corruption before it could spread its tendrils any further.

"Go in quiet. Take out the guards before they know what hit them," I whispered, guiding my team through the shadows. Rashid nodded, his face set in a mask of determination, while Andria checked her weapons, her resolve clear in her focused gaze. Amir, silent and efficient, moved with a grace that belied his years.

Without warning, the silence shattered, and a bullet sliced through the night, grazing my arm. "Ambush!" I yelled as we scattered for cover.

The ensuing firefight was a stark reminder of Nixon's preparedness. He had anticipated our arrival, his guards well-trained and heavily armed. Yet, we were undeterred, our response a testament to our desperation and determination, our bullets singing songs of defiance.

With controlled fury, Rashid laid down covering fire, allowing Andria and Amir to advance strategically. "Eugene, now!" he bellowed, and I surged forward, the gap to the stronghold's entrance rapidly closing.

The door succumbed to our explosives, and we stormed inside, the ensuing chaos scattering Nixon's forces. Our purpose was clear, driving us forward.

At the command center, Nixon awaited, unnervingly calm. "Eugene," he greeted as though we were mere acquaintances rather than adversaries.

Our confrontation was swift; Nixon's strength was in strategy, not combat. Yet, when he fell, the true cost of our victory was laid bare. The stronghold was booby-trapped, a final vindictive act from Nixon we narrowly escaped. The explosion that rocked the dawn sky was a beacon of our pyrrhic victory.

In the aftermath, as we stood among the ruins of what had once been Nixon's seat of power, the toll of our battle was evident. Andria was wounded, a piece of shrapnel marking her sacrifice. Amir's injuries were compounded, pain etched across his young face. Rashid, though physically unscathed, bore the weight of our battle on his soul.

"We did it," I stated, the words tasting of ash. Victory had never felt so hollow. We had eradicated Nixon's threat. The city might have been saved from one tyrant, but the demons we battled seemed only to deepen with each victory.

As we looked towards the horizon, where the first light of dawn promised a new day, I pondered the road ahead. The fight for the city's soul was far from over, and the war against the encroaching darkness would demand more from us than ever before. But together, we were prepared to face whatever challenges lay ahead, united in our resolve to pay the price of victory, no matter how steep.

Chapter 13: Expanding our horizons

The sun's first light painted the skyline in hues of gold and crimson, a stark contrast to the smoldering ruins of Nixon's stronghold behind us. We stood in silence, each lost in thought, the weight of the night's events pressing down on us. The city around us was waking, oblivious to the battle that had raged in its heart.

"We've done what we set out to do here," I began, breaking the silence. My voice sounded foreign to my ears, wearied from the night's exertions. "Nixon's gone, his network disrupted. But this fight... it's bigger than we thought."

Rashid nodded, his eyes scanning the horizon. "The city's just the beginning. With Nixon out, there'll be a power vacuum. Others will try to rise."

Andria, her wound bandaged but her spirit undiminished, added, "And what about Reagan? He's still out there, pulling strings from the shadows."

I turned to face them, the early morning light casting long shadows on the ground.

"We've been reactive for too long, fighting back against the demons in our city. It's time we take the fight to them, to Reagan and whatever network Nixon was a part of."

Amir's gaze was steady, his youthful face set in a resolve far beyond his years. "How do we even start? Reagan's not going to be easy to find, let alone take down."

"We start by expanding our horizons,"

I said my mind racing with the enormity of the task ahead. "We've got allies, people who've been fighting their own battles against the same shadows. It's time we unite share information and resources. Alone, we're just a thorn in their side. Together, we can be the sword."

The idea was daunting. Moving from the shadows of our city to the global stage was a leap into the unknown. Yet, as I looked at my team, I saw the reflection of my own determination mirrored in their eyes.

"We'll need to be smart and strategic," Andria said, her analytical mind already turning over the possibilities. "Reagan's network is going to be extensive, well-protected. We'll need to find its weak points, exploit them."

Rashid stepped forward, his presence grounding. "And we'll need to be prepared for what comes at us. Nixon was just one piece of the puzzle. There are going to be others, maybe even worse."

I nodded, feeling the weight of leadership settle on my shoulders once again. "We will be. We've faced down the darkness in our city and come out stronger. We can do this: take the fight to Reagan, to anyone who threatens the light we're fighting to protect."

The decision was made. Our fight was evolving, moving beyond the confines of our city to a battle that spanned borders and oceans. The road ahead would be fraught with danger, but as the sun rose higher, illuminating the path before us, I felt a surge of hope.

This was more than a new chapter; it was a whole new horizon.

"We do this together," I affirmed, meeting each of their gazes in turn. "For the city, for the innocent lives caught in the crossfire, and for the future we're fighting to secure."

As we turned to leave the ruins of Nixon's stronghold behind, stepping into the light of a new day, I knew the battle ahead would test us in ways we could scarcely imagine. But together, united in purpose and resolve, we were ready to face whatever challenges lay ahead, expand our horizons, and fight back against the darkness, wherever it may lie.

Chapter 14: Whispers from the South

The dawn painted the skyline in strokes of gold and crimson as we regrouped in the shadow of what had been Hoover Nixon's fortress of corruption. Despite the victory, a palpable unease lingered among us, a silent acknowledgment of the battle's cost and the war that lay ahead. The city stirred, blissfully unaware of the night's strife, as a new day broke over the horizon.

It was in this moment of wary anticipation that Danny Watts found us. A young Cleveland police officer with a reputation for integrity in an ocean of corruption, his arrival marked a turning point, the first ripple of the gathering storm.

"Eugene," he began, his voice carrying the weight of unspoken truths, "I've come because I've seen what lies in the shadows, the corruption that festers in the heart of the department... and beyond. My brother, Jax, a reporter in New Harrison, has uncovered evidence of Reagan's reach, a network that spans not just cities but nations."

Rashid, always the protector, eyed Danny with a mix of skepticism and curiosity. "And why bring this to us?" He challenged the inherent distrust of the police, a hard-won instinct among our ranks.

Danny's gaze never wavered, his resolve shining through. "Because you're doing what we can't. You're fighting the shadows, and we're only just beginning to understand. And because of my brother's findings... they could change everything."

Andria, leaning against the remnants of the night's battle, interjected her tone sharp with strategic thought. "What kind of information are we talking about?"

"Detailed accounts of Reagan's operations, connections, and evidence that could expose the entire network. He's ready to publish, but he's being watched and followed. I came to you because I believe, together, we can bring this to light," Danny explained, his earnestness bridging the gap of distrust.

I stepped forward, feeling the larger puzzle pieces falling into place. "And you trust us with this?" I asked, the magnitude of Danny's trust not lost on me.

"Because you're fighting for what's right. And because this is bigger than any of us," Danny replied a simple truth that resonated deep within us.

The room fell silent, the weight of Danny's words settling among us. His brother's evidence was not just a lead but a beacon, illuminating the path ahead. Our fight had grown beyond the underworld of Cleveland, touching the lives of countless others ensnared by Reagan's web.

"Alright, Danny. Let's hear what your brother Jax has," I decided, extending my hand in solidarity, a gesture that marked our collective resolve.

As Danny detailed his brother's discoveries, the scope of our battle widened the stakes elevating with each piece of shared information. The network was vast, its roots entangled in the very fabric of our society, manipulating from the shadows.

"We need to get this evidence out, protect your brother, and dismantle Reagan's network," Andria concluded, her mind already racing with potential strategies.

Considering the logistical challenge, Rashid added, "We're going to need a solid plan, something to draw out Reagan's forces and expose the network."

I felt the burden of leadership heavy on my shoulders as I looked at my team, their faces set in determination. "We'll do it. We'll take the fight to Reagan, unravel his network, and shine a light on the darkness he's spread."

Danny nodded, a silent vow exchanged in the dim light of our hideout. "I'll arrange a meeting with my brother. He knows safe ways to communicate, to stay hidden."

As he left, vanishing into the dawning day, the full gravity of our undertaking dawned on us. This was more than a battle; it was a war for truth and justice against a darkness that spanned continents.

"We dive into the storm together,"

I affirmed, the resolve in my voice mirroring the fire in our hearts. "For the city, the innocent, and the future we're fighting to reclaim."

The sun crested the horizon, a new day born from the night's chaos. The path ahead was fraught with peril, the enemy vast and shadowed. But together, we were a force unto ourselves, a pillar of hope in the gathering storm. Our fight had expanded, our horizons broadened, but our resolve remained unshaken. We were ready to face the coming storm, to stand against the darkness, wherever it may hide.

Epilogue: Dirty South Dreaming

In the quiet hours before dawn, Cleveland lay draped in a serene calm, the turmoil that had churned beneath its surface, now a chapter slowly closing behind us. Atop one of the city's modest skyscrapers, I stood alone, gazing out over the urban expanse that had been both a battlefield and home.

The fight against Nixon and the subsequent unveiling of Donald Reagan's global network marked a turning point, not just for us but for the very nature of our struggle. Danny Watts, a light of integrity in a sea of corruption, had brought us information and a mission far beyond Cleveland's boundaries.

The evidence provided by Danny and his brother Jax had ignited a spark, rallying allies once hidden in the shadows to our cause. A diverse coalition was forming, united by the shared purpose of dismantling Reagan's empire, its roots extending far beyond our city, across states, and into the heart of New Harrison—a city straddling the line between Tennessee and Arkansas, now the next stage in our campaign.

As the first light of dawn began to paint the sky, thoughts of New Harrison filled my mind. The city promised a new battleground and a nexus of Reagan's influence in the South. Our next steps were clear. We would take the fight to him, leveraging the network we had built, and the alliances forged in the fires of our battles in Cleveland.

The early morning air was cool, a gentle breeze carrying the promise of the journey ahead. New Harrison awaited its secrets and challenges, a mystery we were determined to unravel. The road South would not be easy, fraught with known and unforeseen dangers, but the resolve that had carried us this far would see us through.

I turned from the skyline, the city slowly waking below. The time had come to leave Cleveland behind, its streets a testament to our resolve and a reminder of the cost of our fight. The battles we had fought, the allies we had gained, and the darkness we had faced together had prepared us for this moment.

The dawn heralded a new day and a new chapter in our journey. As I made my way down from the rooftop, the city bathed in the soft morning glow, I felt a surge of determination. New Harrison beckoned, and with it, the next phase of our fight.

We were heading into the heart of the South, into the unknown, but we were not the same people who had started this fight. We were stronger, united by a common cause and a shared belief in the light that darkness could never extinguish.

The end of one chapter, the beginning of another. Our journey to New Harrison was not just a move on a strategic map but a declaration that our fight was far from over. Whatever lay ahead, we would face it together, our spirits unyielded, our resolve as unbreakable as ever. In the darkest times, we had discovered our light, and it was in each other, a beacon to guide us through the storms ahead.

THE END

Don't miss out!

Visit the website below and you can sign up to receive emails whenever HooliewoodYella publishes a new book. There's no charge and no obligation.

https://books2read.com/r/B-A-MNLEB-ZANAD

BOOKS 2 READ

Connecting independent readers to independent writers.

Also by HooliewoodYella

Eugene Halif
Eugene Halif
The Order Of The Eclipse

"The Voice of Goodnor"
"THE VOICE OF GOODNOR" The Storm Of Unity' (An
Adventure Through Cain Park)

Standalone
Lost in the Land: The Disappearance" Mike Avignon

About the Author

Martell HoolieWoodYella Daugherty is a self-taught filmmaker, director, and screenwriter whose journey into the realm of film began at the tender age of 11. Born in Berkeley, California, and raised in Cleveland, Ohio, Daugherty's early fascination with cinema set the stage for a career marked by passion, creativity, and a deep-seated love for storytelling. Beyond the confines of film sets and editing rooms, he is an ardent enthusiast of combat sports, reflecting a spirited dedication to both discipline and physical excellence. His affinity for animals and the great outdoors showcases a soul deeply connected to the natural world, while his adventurous spirit often finds him exploring the unknown. Music occupies a special place in Daugherty's life, serving as both inspiration and solace, encapsulating the depth of his artistic sensibility. Above all, cherished moments with family and friends are Daugherty's most valued treasures, underscoring a life enriched by deep, meaningful relationships.